Paw an

Max was concentrating intently on the cellar door. Then he started whining and scrabbling away at the bottom of it. Every muscle in his strong, lean body tensed as he tried with all his might to get it open.

Then the twins froze. A loud, scratching noise was coming from the cellar, right underneath their feet.

Now they knew why Max as making such a fuss.

Titles in Jenny Dale's Police Pup series:

All of Jenny Dale's POLICE PUP books can be ordered at your local bookshop or are available by post from Book Service by Post
(tel: 01624 675137).

Paw and Order

Jenny Dale
Illustrated by Mick Reid

A Working Partners Book

MACMILLAN CHILDREN'S BOOKS

Special thanks to Narinder Dhami

First published 2000 by Macmillan Children's Books
a division of Macmillan Publishers Limited
25 Eccleston Place, London SW1W 9NF
Basingstoke and Oxford
www.macmillan.com

Associated companies throughout the world

Created by Working Partners Limited 2000
London W6 0QT

Police Pup is a trade mark of Working Partners Limited

ISBN 0 330 39371 5

Copyright © Working Partners Limited 2000
Illustrations © Mick Reid 2000

1 3 5 7 9 8 6 4 2

A CIP catalogue record for this book is available from
the British Library.

Typeset by SX Composing DTP, Rayleigh, Essex
Printed and bound in Great Britain by Mackays of Chatham plc, Kent

Many thanks also to
Steve Dean and Peter Whitehead
of the Metropolitan Police Service for their
invaluable advice.

In memory of Metpol Bruno 40
– who served as a fine police dog for ten years.

Chapter One

"This is cool!" said ten-year-old Liam Wilson. He stood in the empty bedroom, looking round with a big grin on his face. The room was large and airy, and it looked out over the village high street, and to the hills of the Peak District beyond.

As Liam stared out of the window, two boys zoomed past on mountain bikes. A large crowd were playing football on the village green, and having a great time by the look of it. Liam's grin grew even wider. Ellandale was so different from the city they had just left. He was going to *love* living here.

Liam spun round as his twin sister Becky burst into the room along with Max, the Wilsons' German shepherd dog. "I want this room," he said quickly.

"Hey, that's not fair!" Becky grumbled, pushing her long, dark hair from her face. "Mum said we had to decide together!"

"Well, I was here first!" Liam argued, pulling a face at his sister. "Wasn't I, Max?"

Max cocked his head to one side and stared solemnly from Becky to Liam with big dark eyes as if he understood perfectly what they were saying.

"Typical!" Becky grumbled, but Liam could tell that she was too excited to be really annoyed. He followed her out, and into the back bedroom.

"Oh, this is brilliant!" Becky exclaimed, her face brightening. Although the room was smaller than Liam's, it had a fantastic view. Lark Cottage had fields behind it, stretching away as far as the eye could see, and a winding river that glittered in the morning sun.

"Maybe I'll take this one instead!" Liam remarked wickedly.

Becky gave him a shove. "You're a pain, Liam Wilson!" she snorted.

Meanwhile, Max was snuffling around in the corner of the room, investigating the scents left behind by the previous owners. His long, plumy tail swished from side to side.

Becky crouched down beside him and stroked his silky ears. "You look at home already, don't you, Max?" She grinned. "I reckon he's going to like it here!"

"So are we!" Liam said confidently. He didn't have to ask if Becky agreed with

him. They were so close that they could almost always guess what the other was thinking. They'd been shocked when their father John Wilson, a policeman, told them he had a new job and they would have to move. But as soon as they'd set eyes on the village of Ellandale in the Derbyshire Dales, they'd begun to change their minds.

Becky ruffled the German shepherd's thick black-and-brown fur. "Max starts work with Dad tomorrow, doesn't he?"

Liam nodded. "Yes, so all the baddies in Ellandale had better watch out!" he joked, sliding an arm round Max's neck.

Max woofed and thumped his tail against the bare floorboards.

The German shepherd was no ordinary family pet. He was a highly trained police dog, and the twins' father was his handler. Max had come to live with the Wilsons when he was just twelve weeks old, and had quickly become one of the family. Now that he had completed his long training course, he would be helping PC Wilson fight crime in his new job around Ellandale.

Max's tail stopped wagging. His ears pricked up and he listened, an alert expression on his face.

A second later the voice of the twins' mother, Tina Wilson, floated up the stairs. "Have you two decided which bedrooms you want yet?"

Liam and Becky both smiled. Even though they were used to Max's amazing ability to stay alert to every sight or sound, it never failed to impress them. The fact that nothing escaped the attention of a German shepherd was one of the reasons why they were in such demand as police dogs.

"Yes, Liam's having the front and I'm having the back!" Becky called.

"Good," said Mrs Wilson, coming into the room. She pushed back a lock of fair hair with a dusty hand. She was a nurse, and could usually be relied on to be super-cool and efficient, but today the stresses of moving house were clearly beginning to get to her. "Now, will you come downstairs so that the removals men can bring the furniture up, please?"

Becky, Liam and Max clattered downstairs as John Wilson came in through the door with yet another large box.

"All right, you two?" he asked with a smile. A tall, well-built man, he seemed very laid-back, but he had an air of calm authority about him.

They both nodded enthusiastically.

"Hey, let's go and check out the back garden!" Becky said, nudging Liam in the ribs, and they ran off down the hallway, Max bounding along beside them.

With its stone floor, old pine cupboards and open fireplace at one end, the kitchen was very different to the modern one in their old house. In fact, the whole cottage with its slightly sloping walls, winding corridors and exposed beams was totally different to the modern semi they had left behind.

"Look." Liam pointed at the back door, which leaned slightly to the left. "It's all crooked!"

"So's this one." Becky stared at a large wooden door in the corner of the kitchen. "I wonder where it goes?"

"Dad said the cellar's down there," Liam told her. "How old do you think the house is?"

"Didn't you see the carved stone over the door when we came in?" Becky asked. She always noticed details like that. "It said Lark Cottage, 1820."

"1820!" Liam was impressed. Then he grinned. "I wonder if it has got a ghost!"

Becky shook her head. "Of course not,"

she said quickly, not liking the idea very much. "Anyway," she added, "if there *are* any ghosts, Max will soon catch them!"

"Max can be our official ghost-catcher!" Liam joked. He glanced down at the dog, and then frowned. "Hey, what's wrong with him?"

Max was concentrating intently on the cellar door. Then he started whining and scrabbling away at the bottom of it, every muscle in his strong, lean body tensed as he tried with all his might to get it open.

"Maybe he's found a ghost already!" Becky joked back.

Then the twins froze. A loud, scratching noise was coming from the cellar, right underneath their feet.

Now they knew why Max was making such a fuss.

Chapter Two

Liam and Becky grabbed each other in fright. Meanwhile, Max redoubled his efforts to get the door open.

"What was *that*?" Liam whispered, his eyes wide.

"Maybe it's a mouse," Becky hissed.

"It'd have to be as big as Max to make that kind of noise!" Liam replied.

They looked at each other.

"Maybe it *is* a ghost!" Liam muttered.

"Don't be stupid," Becky said stoutly.

"We'll just have to go and see for ourselves!" Liam said, reaching for the key which hung on a hook on the wall.

"Maybe we should go and tell Mum and Dad," Becky suggested nervously. Liam was always rushing into situations like this, and it had got them both into trouble more than once.

"We'll take Max," Liam said. "You know he'll look after us."

Becky nodded. Max was fiercely protective of them both, and would never let anything hurt them.

As Liam cautiously pushed the door open, they heard the scratching noise again. This time it was louder.

"Sit, Max!" Becky said sharply as Max attempted to dash down the stairs.

Max immediately sat. His whole body was still, but alert; his ears cocked.

Liam took a firm hold of Max's collar. "OK," he said bravely, "shall we go down?"

"Isn't there a light or something?" Becky asked, peering over Liam's shoulder into the pitch-black, musty darkness.

Liam felt along the wall, and flipped a switch. A dim light came on, but it wasn't really bright enough to light up the whole cellar, which ran the length of the house.

Slowly Liam began to walk down the stairs, Max pressed close against him, and Becky following behind.

They were halfway down when they heard the scratching noise again.

"It's coming from over there!" Becky whispered, pointing to some boxes in the corner. Max was already straining to go in that direction.

Liam let go of Max's collar, and he bounded down the steps, barking loudly. An answering woof made Liam and Becky glance at each other in surprise.

Next moment, a little brown-and-white Jack Russell terrier popped out of one of the boxes and barked cheekily at them, its stumpy tail wagging.

"It's a dog!" Liam exclaimed.

"Oh, what a shame!" Becky grinned. "I was really looking forward to meeting the ghost of Lark Cottage!"

The dog scrambled out of the box, and he and Max introduced themselves by sniffing cautiously at each other. Then the dog ran over to Liam and Becky and danced around their ankles, barking merrily while they stroked him.

"I wonder where he's come from?" Liam said, laughing as the overexcited terrier ran round in circles trying to catch its own tail. "Do you think he's a stray?"

Becky shook her head. "He's got an identity tag on." She bent down and picked the Jack Russell up. But it was hard to read the tag while he was enthusiastically giving her face a good wash. "Stop it!" Becky giggled. "Come on, we'd better go and tell Mum and Dad."

"Becky! Liam!" Right at that moment they heard their mother's voice overhead in the kitchen. "What on earth are you doing in the cellar?"

"You'll never guess!" Becky called back as they all hurried upstairs.

As they came out into the kitchen, Tina Wilson turned to them with a smile. She had two people with her, a fair-haired woman carrying a delicious-smelling pie, and a girl of about the same age as the twins, who also had fair hair. "Becky, Liam, I want you to meet our new neighbours. This is Mrs Gibbs and her daughter Julie—" Then she stopped, her eyes widening. "Where on *earth* did that dog come from?"

"Well—" Becky began, but she didn't get a chance to say anything more.

Julie saw the dog in Becky's arms and rushed over. "Scooter, you naughty boy! I've been looking for you everywhere!"

Scooter yapped joyfully as Julie took him from Becky.

"Is he yours?" Liam asked. "He was in our cellar."

"So that's where he's been going!" Julie exclaimed.

"Our cellar runs alongside yours so there must be a hole in the wall somewhere," Julie's mother said. "I'll get my husband to check, and block it up."

"We thought it was a ghost!" Becky grinned.

"No, it was just Scooter's way of welcoming you to Ellandale! " Julie laughed.

"And that's why we're here too, even though Scooter got in ahead of us!" Mrs Gibbs handed Tina Wilson the dish. "I was doing some baking, and thought you might appreciate an apple pie."

"How kind!" Mrs Wilson said gratefully. "It smells delicious. That's dessert sorted out for later!"

"Is this your dog?" Julie asked the twins, looking down at Max who was sitting quietly next to them. "He's beautiful."

"Yes, Max is a really special dog," Liam said proudly. "He works with our dad. He's a policeman."

"I know," Julie said. "Everyone in the village knows about Max. We were told about it at the Neighbourhood Watch meeting. We're all really excited!"

"Did you hear that, Max?" Becky said, patting the German shepherd's head. Max nuzzled her hand with his cold black nose. "You're famous already!"

"Maybe your dad could give me a few tips on how to train Scooter!" Julie sighed, struggling to prevent the terrier from chewing the neck of her T-shirt. "Are you starting at Ellandale Primary School tomorrow?"

Liam nodded. "We're in 6K – Miss Kendall's class."

Julie's face lit up. "So am I!"

"Oh, great!" Becky was pleased too. She already liked Julie a lot. "What's Miss Kendall like?"

"Oh, she's cool!" Julie assured them. "She's a bit strict, but she can be a good laugh too."

"Come on, Julie." Mrs Gibbs beckoned to her daughter. "Let's get out of our new neighbours' way, so that they can finish their unpacking."

"OK, Mum." Julie grinned at Liam and Becky. "See you tomorrow!"

"Well, that's our first friend in Ellandale," Becky said happily as Julie and her mum went home.

Liam nodded. "And it looks like Max has made a friend too," he said, as Max watched Scooter head off next door. "Is it time for lunch yet, Mum?" he asked.

Mrs Wilson groaned. "I can't even think about cooking at the moment! Why don't you take Max for a quick walk along the lane, and then we'll send your dad out for a takeaway?"

"Great!" The twins rushed to get Max's lead, and soon they were unlatching the gate at the bottom of the long, overgrown garden. After living in London, where the view from their garden was another row of houses, it was odd now to see a field with woodlands beyond.

"Don't be too long, and keep in sight of the house!" their mum called.

"Mum never liked us taking Max out for walks on our own when we lived in London," Becky remarked.

"Well, the country's different, isn't it?"

Liam replied. "There's not so much traffic for one thing. It's a lot safer."

Becky sighed happily. "It's going to be great living here! Everyone's so friendly—" She broke off suddenly as Max stopped dead in his tracks and stiffened.

Liam stared down at him. "What's wrong, boy?" he asked.

Max was staring at a large clump of bushes. Every hair on his body seemed to bristle with tension as he stood as still as a stone.

"There's something in those bushes!" Becky whispered urgently.

"Is someone there?" Liam called, trying not to sound nervous. "If there is, you'd better come out now!"

There was a rustling in the bushes, and Liam and Becky tensed as Max growled. Who – or what – had he found this time?

Chapter Three

A second later, the bushes parted, and a boy stepped out. He had tousled brown hair, and wore old jeans and a baggy T-shirt.

Liam and Becky stared at him.

"You nearly scared us to death!" Becky cried.

"Sorry," the boy muttered, keeping a wary eye on Max.

"It's OK, he won't hurt you," Liam said quickly. "He was just trying to protect us. It's all right, Max. Friend." He looked at the boy. "Just hold out your hand so he

21

can get your scent." German shepherd dogs are usually suspicious of strangers, which is one of the reasons why they make such good police dogs.

The boy did as Liam said. Max sniffed at him with interest, accepted that the boy was no danger to Liam and Becky and sat down quietly on his haunches.

"What were you doing in the bushes?" Becky asked curiously.

"Nothing," the boy muttered. "I lost something, that's all."

Liam thought that was a pretty lame excuse, but he didn't get a chance to say anything as Becky chimed in again.

"What's your name? How old are you? Do you live in Ellandale?" she quizzed.

The boy looked down at his feet. "I'm Paul, and I'm ten. We've just moved to Ellandale."

"So have we!" Becky exclaimed, delighted. "I'm Becky and this is my twin brother Liam. You must be going to Ellandale Primary School too. Are you in Miss Kendall's class?"

"Er – Maybe . . ." Paul muttered.

Liam wondered why Paul looked so uncomfortable, although he was trying to hide it by stroking Max.

Paul noticed Liam staring at him, and

flushed. "I've got a dog too," he muttered.

"Oh, what's it called?" Becky asked with interest. "And what kind is it?"

Paul shrugged. "He's a mongrel called Bouncer."

"You'll have to bring him over to meet Max," Becky said happily. "Then we can all go out for walks!"

"I can't!" Paul said quickly. Then he added, "I mean, Bouncer's staying with . . . someone else at the moment – until we've settled in."

Liam wondered why Paul looked so miserable when he said that. Maybe it was just because he missed his dog so much. Liam couldn't help feeling sorry for him. "I bet you miss him. Why don't you walk home with us and Max – you can stay for lunch if you want?" he suggested.

Paul's face lit up. "Could I?"

"Sure!" Liam said. "Mum won't mind – but perhaps you need to tell yours?"

Paul shook his head quickly. "No . . . my mum won't mind either," he mumbled.

"Great!" Liam beamed. "Come on!"

Becky secretly thought that their mum might well mind as she was so busy, but there was no stopping Liam once he got an idea into his head.

As they headed back to the cottage, Liam couldn't help noticing that Paul didn't say very much, but he really seemed to like being with Max. Maybe he was just shy – and missing his own dog.

"Hi, you lot." Their father was in the kitchen putting on his fleece when they arrived home. "I'm just off to fetch pizzas." He smiled at Paul. "Who's this?"

"Paul," Paul muttered, shuffling his feet.

John Wilson raised an eyebrow at him, and eventually the boy added, "Carter. Paul Carter."

"He's just moved to Ellandale and Liam's invited him for lunch," Becky informed her father as her mother hurried into the kitchen.

"Getting into friendly country ways already, are we?" her father teased as he went out.

"So where do you live, Paul?" Tina Wilson asked as she hunted around in one of the cardboard boxes for some plates. "Becky, can you find some glasses?"

"Oh, over the other side of Ellandale," Paul said vaguely.

"Whereabouts exactly?" But Tina didn't wait for an answer. "Try that box over there, Becky. I'll be so glad when we've finally got everything organized!"

"What do your mum and dad do, Paul?" Becky asked.

Liam noticed that Paul turned a little red at the question.

"My dad's a journalist," he said reluctantly. "Mum's an accountant."

"Maybe we can meet them tomorrow," Mrs Wilson suggested, putting a bottle of lemonade on the table.

Paul didn't answer, and Liam could see that he looked relieved as Becky began to chatter on about how brilliant Ellandale was. He plonked himself down next to Max and sat gently ruffling the German shepherd's fur.

"Oh good – food at last!" said Tina Wilson as the front door eventually slammed twenty minutes later.

"Here we are," PC Wilson said, hurrying into the kitchen with a stack of pizza boxes. "And I've brought someone to meet you all." He turned to smile at the young policewoman who came into the room behind him. "This is WPC Janie Blake. She's going to be working with me at the station."

"Hi, everyone," Janie said. She had bright red hair and a wide smile, and looked very friendly.

But as everyone said hello, Liam glanced at Paul. All the colour had drained out of his face.

"And this must be Max!" Janie went over to the German shepherd, who was lying under the table, resting his head on Becky's feet. Once he had sniffed at Janie and checked her over, Max wagged his tail and allowed her to stroke him.

"Have you got any pets?" Becky asked.

Janie grinned at her. "Well . . . only

my snake, Copper!"

"A snake!" Becky's eyes widened.

"You can come over and see him if you like," Janie told her.

"Would you like to join us for lunch, Janie?" Mrs Wilson was busy cutting up the pizzas. "We've certainly got enough!"

"I'd love to," Janie replied, "but I'm on duty. I just happened to meet John on my

beat." Reluctantly she went over to the door. "If Jim finds out I'm slacking, he won't be too pleased!"

"That's Sergeant Jim Thornton," the twins' father explained. "He's the desk sergeant at the station, so he's based there most of the time."

"She's nice," Becky said as Janie said her goodbyes and left. "But then, *everyone's* nice here!"

"I hope not!" Liam snorted, "or Dad and Max won't have much to do!"

Becky stuck her tongue out at him. "What's Sergeant Thornton like?" she asked.

"Oh, I hear he's a good police officer," their father replied, picking up a large slice of pizza. "But I think it's going to take a bit of time for him to get used to Max!"

A few moments later, Liam glanced

across at Paul again, and could hardly believe his eyes. The others had barely started, but Paul had finished his first slice of pizza and was already reaching for a second one. It was as though he hadn't eaten for days.

When Paul had demolished a fourth slice, he hurriedly pushed his plate away. "Thanks, Mrs Wilson, that was great," he gabbled. "I've got to go now."

"Don't you want to stay and have some apple pie?" Becky asked. "Our neighbour, Mrs Gibbs, made it."

Paul hesitated.

"Yes, do stay," Mrs Wilson urged. "You still haven't told us much about your parents, or where you live."

Paul looked uncomfortable again. "Sorry, I can't," he said abruptly. "Thanks again. Bye." He hurried over to the back door, and was gone.

"Well!" Becky sniffed. "That wasn't very friendly, was it?"

"Poor boy. Maybe he's got some problems at home." Mrs Wilson frowned, then turned to her husband. "John, we'd better get on with the unpacking."

"There's something funny going on with that Paul," Liam whispered to Becky.

Becky nodded. "He didn't seem to want to tell us much about himself, did he?"

"And then when Janie came in, he looked really scared, like he'd seen a ghost!" Liam added.

Becky frowned. "I wonder why? Do you think he's in some sort of trouble?"

"I don't know," Liam shrugged. "But maybe we can find out at school tomorrow."

Chapter Four

"I wonder how Max is getting on?" Liam said as he slung his school bag over his shoulder. "After all, it's *his* first day too!"

It was the next morning, and the twins were walking to school with Julie. PC Wilson and Max were working an early shift, and had left before Liam and Becky had even got out of bed.

"Max will be fine!" Becky said, as the three of them walked across the village green. "Isn't it a lovely day?"

The sun was shining again, and the ducks were splashing around in the pond.

In the distance they could see the hills of the Peak District, shrouded in a thin mist.

"Wait until the winter," Julie told them. "We usually get snowed in. Once we couldn't get to school for three days!"

"Cool!" Liam said, as they arrived at school.

Liam and Becky had visited Ellandale Primary School at the end of last term, so they had already seen the old Victorian building with its red-tiled roof. It was very different from their old school, which was modern and open-plan.

"I wonder how all our old schoolfriends are getting on," Becky said as they walked through the playground gates. "We could e-mail some of them this weekend."

Liam wasn't listening. He'd just spotted something very interesting going on across the playground. "Hey, Becky, look!

There's Max – and Dad too!"

Sure enough, at the far end of the playground stood Max and PC Wilson. The twins' father was deep in conversation with a tall, dark-haired woman who wore silver-framed glasses.

Becky recognized her as Mrs Mason, the head teacher, whom they'd met when they'd looked around the school. "What

on *earth* are they doing here?" she asked, puzzled.

"Well, there's only one way to find out!" Liam raced off across the playground. Becky and Julie followed.

Max had already spotted the twins in the distance, but because he was on duty, he showed no reaction, apart from wagging his tail very slightly.

" . . . and we'll certainly do our best to get to the bottom of this," PC Wilson was saying. Then he smiled. "Hello, you two. I thought we might see you this morning."

"Hi, Dad, what's going on?" Liam asked breathlessly. He and Becky didn't touch Max. They knew better than to do that while he was on duty.

"Good morning, Rebecca and Liam," Mrs Mason said pointedly. "Welcome to Ellandale Primary."

Liam blushed. "Good morning, Mrs Mason," he muttered.

"Good morning, Mrs Mason," Becky said. But she couldn't help grinning. Not many people managed to put Liam off when he was determined to find out what was going on!

PC Wilson glanced at the head teacher. "You did say that you were going to tell the pupils about the thefts, didn't you, Mrs Mason?"

Mrs Mason nodded. "Yes, in assembly this morning."

"Well, there's no harm in you three knowing then," PC Wilson went on. "It seems that some food which was recently delivered to the school has been stolen."

"What kind of food?" Liam asked.

"Biscuits, and milk for the staffroom, and crisps and chocolate for the school shop," Mrs Mason said grimly. "They went missing while the delivery man was unpacking his van in the playground."

"So Max and I are here to investigate," PC Wilson explained.

"Well, I do hope you find out who took them," said Mrs Mason, as she glanced at her watch. "I must go. School starts in five minutes." She turned to leave, then stopped. "Perhaps you and Max would like to come to an assembly sometime, and talk to our pupils?" Mrs Mason glanced at the large crowd of children that was gathering to stare at the dog. "I know they'd be very interested!"

"We'd love to," PC Wilson said, smiling. "How about Wednesday?"

Mrs Mason nodded, then hurried off.

The crowd of children edged forward for a closer look at Ellandale's new police dog. Max sat obediently next to his handler, not letting his noisy audience distract him. Liam and Becky grinned at each other. Max always attracted attention wherever he went!

"Can we say goodbye to Max, Dad?" Becky asked, as the bell rang for the start of the school day. Her father nodded.

As the twins knelt down to fuss over Max, the German shepherd glanced up at his handler to confirm that this was all right while he was on duty. When he saw that it was, his tail began to wag like crazy. He pressed against Liam and Becky, rubbing his head against Liam as playfully as a puppy.

Julie also gave the police dog a pat. "Max is so clever!" she said admiringly as they ran over to line up. "I bet he'll find that thief, no problem!"

"Of course he will!" Liam agreed, as they joined the rest of the class.

"I just hope the thief's left some chocolate for us to buy at playtime!" Becky joked.

A slim, brown-haired woman was waiting for everyone to stop chattering and be still. It was Miss Kendall, Becky and Liam's teacher. She gave a signal for the girl at the front of the line to lead everyone into their new classroom.

"Hello, Liam, hello, Becky," she said, smiling as they passed. "I see Julie's already taking care of you," Miss Kendall went on. "You can sit together in class if you like."

"Oh, Miss Kendall, can Paul Carter sit with us as well?" Liam asked. "He's a new boy too."

Miss Kendall looked surprised. "Well, he's not in my class," she said. "You and Becky are my only new pupils this term."

"That's odd." Liam frowned as they filed into the classroom.

Becky looked just as puzzled.

"You must have made a mistake," said Miss Kendall.

Chapter Five

"It's really *weird* about Paul, isn't it?" Liam remarked as he and Becky walked up to the front door of Lark Cottage. They'd just finished their first day at Ellandale Primary, and all in all, it had gone OK.

Becky nodded. "Sure is. How come he hasn't been registered at Ellandale Primary if he's living here now?" She unlocked the front door and pushed it open. Then she laughed. "Hi, Max! You must have heard us coming, as usual!"

Max was waiting eagerly behind the front door, woofing a welcome and looking very pleased to see them. He pawed impatiently at the carpet until both Becky and Liam had dropped their schoolbags and begun to fuss over him.

"Dad must be home," Liam said as he rumpled Max's thick coat.

"No, he had to go to a meeting at another police station after he finished his shift," said Mrs Wilson, coming out of the living room. "Hello, you two. How was your first day?"

"OK," Liam and Becky said together.

Liam stuck his head inside the living room to see what his mum had been doing. He whistled. "Hey, Mum, this looks great!" The boxes had been unpacked, the curtains had been put up, and all the furniture was now in place – although when he tried to switch the TV on, he was disappointed to see that no one had tuned it in yet.

He followed Becky into the kitchen, where their mum was in the middle of unpacking more boxes. The radio news was on:

"Police are becoming increasingly concerned for the safety of a young boy who disappeared from his home in Buxton two days ago . . ."

Then the radio report was drowned out by a hopeful-sounding woof from Max. Liam turned to see his mother holding Max's lead. "Dad said you can take Max out for a walk if you like," she said.

Max sat, ears pricked at the word "walk", tail thump-thumping on the carpet. His warm brown gaze switched from one twin to the other, pleading for one of them to put his lead on.

"Actually, if you're taking Max out now, perhaps I'll pop along and see Dr Fenwick," Mrs Wilson said. She reached out and turned off the radio. "I need to confirm which patients I'll be visiting when I start work." The twins' mum was the new district nurse for Ellandale and the surrounding area, but her job didn't start for a few more days. "We'll have tea when you get back, OK?"

"Let's go the same way we went yesterday," Liam suggested, as they began their walk. "We might meet Paul again."

Becky nodded. "OK."

They went exactly the same route, letting Max have a good, long run in the fields.

There was no sign of Paul.

But when they were about to head for home, Becky suddenly grabbed Liam's arm. "Look, there he is!"

Paul was wandering along the lane in

front of them. Liam yelled, "Paul! Wait!" as loudly as he could.

Paul glanced round, and, seeing it was Liam and Becky, he stopped – though he didn't look particularly pleased to see them.

Liam thought Paul looked really tired – and a bit scruffy.

"Hi!" Becky said breezily. "We were hoping to see you. Why weren't you at school today?"

Paul blinked. "Oh . . . I . . . I couldn't come," he muttered.

"Why not?" Liam demanded.

"We're still unpacking and settling in," Paul replied. He shuffled his muddy trainers. "I'll probably start next week."

"You're not on our class register though," Liam argued, puzzled. And though he didn't say anything, he didn't think much of Paul's excuse for not starting school today, like him and Becky. After all, they'd only just moved to Ellandale too!

"Oh . . ." Paul cleared his throat. "The school must have made a mistake . . . Look, I've got to go home now."

"Maybe we could come with you," Becky suggested. "We could help you unpack, and we could meet Bouncer—"

"No," Paul snapped – rather rudely, Becky thought. "We're going out shopping soon, so I've got to get home." And he ran off.

Liam nudged Becky. "Do you think we should go after him? Max can follow his scent!"

"No, Mum'll go crazy if we're late home," Becky said firmly.

"But there's definitely something odd going on," Liam grumbled.

"You're just nosy, that's all!" Becky grinned at him. "But maybe we should tell Dad about Paul."

"Right," Liam agreed.

They took Max home by a different route, going into the village instead of cutting through their back garden.

As they walked up the high street, they saw the police station on their left. A balding, middle-aged man in uniform was standing by the noticeboard outside, taking down some of the old posters. He had a new rolled-up one under his arm.

Becky nudged Liam. "Hey, look. Do you reckon that's Sergeant Thornton?"

"There's only one way to find out," Liam replied.

The man glanced up as the twins and Max went over to him.

"Hello, are you Sergeant Thornton?"

Becky asked.

The man nodded.

Becky beamed. "We're Liam and Becky Wilson. And you must have met Max."

"Oh, hello," Sergeant Thornton said gruffly. "Your dad's not here. He's gone to a meeting."

"Yes, we know," Liam said cheerfully. "We just thought we'd say hello."

Sergeant Thornton didn't look very impressed. He continued taking down the posters, frowning at Max as he did so.

"Don't you like dogs, Sergeant Thornton?" Liam asked.

Becky grinned to herself as Sergeant Thornton looked rather uncomfortable. Liam didn't have any problem with putting people on the spot!

"I reckon we've managed well enough in Ellandale without a police dog in the

past," Sergeant Thornton muttered, unrolling the poster under his arm.

Liam opened his mouth to argue, but Becky clutched his arm before he could speak.

"Liam!" she cried. "Look!"

The poster's headline read: MISSING: HAVE YOU SEEN THIS BOY? And underneath it was a large photograph – of Paul.

Chapter Six

"Paul Carter disappeared from his home in Buxton two days ago," Becky read aloud. "Paul is ten years old and has brown hair and blue eyes. If anyone has any information about his current whereabouts, please contact any local police station immediately."

Sergeant Thornton had finished pinning the poster up, and was heading back into the station. Liam, Becky and Max raced after him.

"Sergeant Thornton!" Liam panted.

"What is it now?" Sergeant Thornton

sighed crossly.

"That boy on the poster!" Liam gasped. "We've seen him!"

"Twice!" Becky added.

Sergeant Thornton stared at them suspiciously. "Are you sure?" he asked, as a police car swept onto the forecourt and drew to a halt.

"Oh, look! It's Dad!" Becky cried, relieved. Their father would believe them. After all, he'd met Paul himself yesterday.

"What's going on here?" John Wilson asked as the twins and Max ran over to him, followed by Sergeant Thornton.

"Dad, that boy who's missing – it's Paul!" Becky gabbled urgently.

"What?" PC Wilson looked puzzled as he leant over and said hello to Max. "I'd heard that there was a boy missing, but I haven't seen any of the details yet."

"Look, Dad!" Liam pointed at the poster. "It's Paul!"

His father stared. "Good grief! That's the boy who came to lunch yesterday – I thought there was something odd about him!" He turned to Sergeant Thornton. "So what's the story, Jim?"

"Paul's parents reported him missing to Buxton Police Station yesterday," Sergeant Thornton explained. "They think he must have sneaked out the night before because his bed hadn't been slept in."

"Any idea why he ran away?" PC Wilson asked.

"His parents think it might be because of the family dog," Sergeant Thornton replied. "Apparently they decided to take it to an animal shelter for re-homing. They're both very busy people, and found the dog too much work. It was pretty destructive around the house."

Liam looked at Becky.

"Bouncer!" he said. "Dad, Paul told us he had a dog, but he didn't say it had been given away!"

PC Wilson looked at Liam and Becky. "When was the last time you two saw Paul?" he asked urgently.

"Just now," Liam explained. "When we took Max for a walk."

"You'd better take me to the exact spot," PC Wilson said. He took Max's lead from Liam. "Max might be able to find him, if it wasn't too long ago."

"There's a search party being organized for tonight," Jim Thornton added.

Liam and Becky glanced at each other. They knew that the police often conducted searches at night-time. There were fewer people around then, so there was more chance for police dogs to pick up the scent of the missing person.

Their father had explained to them before that when people like Paul were missing and feeling scared and alone, their body gave off scents that a highly trained police dog could pick up on.

"OK, let's go." PC Wilson hurried off with Max trotting beside him.

"Imagine running away from home!" Becky shivered as they all went up the street. "I wonder where Paul's been sleeping?"

"In the fields, probably," Liam replied. "No wonder he looked a bit of a mess last time we saw him."

They both fell silent as they ran to catch up with Max and their father.

"Paul might have moved on, of course," PC Wilson said as they reached the lane where the twins had seen Paul. "But if we're lucky, he might still be around this area." He released the German shepherd from his lead, and said, "Max, find him!"

Max set off along the lane, sniffing the air, his eyes bright and alert. Nothing distracted him as he concentrated on the search for the missing boy.

PC Wilson, Liam and Becky followed. They all searched until dusk began to fall, but there was no sign of the runaway boy.

After an hour or so, PC Wilson gave up. "Come on, you two," he called. "We'd better get home. Your mum's going to be wondering where we are. There'll be a proper search party out tonight anyway."

"Poor Paul." Becky shivered as they headed homewards. "It's getting chilly."

"Yes, we're in for a cold snap over-night." PC Wilson looked worried. "Let's hope we find Paul before it's too late."

Chapter Seven

"PAUL!" Liam yelled at the top of his voice. "WHERE ARE YOU?"

"Oh, shut up, Liam!" Becky clapped her hands over her ears. "This isn't working!"

It was the following afternoon. The twins had just arrived home from school, and had gone straight out into the countryside again to look for the missing boy. A search party, including PC Wilson and Max, had been out searching the previous night, but they hadn't found any trace of Paul.

If Max hadn't managed to find anything, Becky didn't really see what she and Liam could do, but Liam was determined to try, and Becky had gone along with him, as usual.

"He's got to be here *somewhere*," Liam wailed, frustrated.

"Yes, but if he knows everyone's looking for him, he won't come out, will he?" Becky said sensibly.

Everyone at school had been talking about the missing boy earlier that day. Liam and Becky had asked loads of people if they'd seen Paul. But surprisingly, nobody had.

"Well, he must have found a good hiding-place if *no one's* seen him," Liam remarked. "But where?"

Becky glanced at her watch. "Look, we'd better go," she said. "Mum said to be home by six, and it's getting dark, anyway. I just hope Paul's safe and warm wherever he is," she sighed.

Liam nodded, but secretly he didn't think there was much chance of that.

When the twins arrived home, they were surprised to see that Sergeant Thornton was there, having a mug of tea in the kitchen with their parents.

"Has Paul turned up, Dad?" Liam asked hopefully.

"I'm afraid not," his father replied. "We did find evidence that someone had been camping out in a field at the back of our garden, but it looks as if they've moved on. Perhaps it was Paul."

Max was lying under the kitchen table, one eye open, and one closed. Liam noticed that Sergeant Thornton was keeping a wary eye on him as he slowly drank his tea.

"Did you find out any more about

Paul's dog, Dad?" Becky asked.

PC Wilson nodded. "Apparently his parents were told by the animal shelter that Bouncer had been re-homed in Ellandale."

"So *that's* why Paul came here!" Liam exclaimed. "Have you spoken to Bouncer's new owner, Dad?"

"Yes, her name's Mrs Castle," PC Wilson replied. "We interviewed her in case she'd seen Paul hanging about, but no luck – she hasn't."

"Did you see Bouncer?" Becky wanted to know.

"Yes, I did, and poor old Bouncer didn't look too happy either!" PC Wilson said, sighing. "I'd guess he's missing Paul just as much as Paul's missing him."

"So what happens now, Dad?" Liam asked.

"We've brought in some extra police officers for tonight, and we'll carry on searching then," said their father. "Hopefully we'll find him before too long."

"Searching the countryside isn't easy," Sergeant Thornton said as he finished his tea. "If someone doesn't want to be found, there's not much you can do."

"Well, I'm sure Max will help." PC Wilson leaned under the table and patted Max's flanks.

Sergeant Thornton sniffed. "I suppose dogs have got their uses," he remarked shortly. "Some of the time anyway." He stood up. "Time I was going. Thanks for the tea, Mrs Wilson," he said.

"He's a bit grumpy, isn't he?" Becky whispered as their mum showed Sergeant Thornton to the door. "And he doesn't seem to like animals much either!"

Her father began to clear away the empty mugs. "I think he's just a bit set in his ways, that's all."

"Will you and Max still be coming to our assembly tomorrow, Dad?" Becky asked. "Or will you be too busy?"

"Oh, we'll come," her father replied. "It won't take very long, and besides, it's a good opportunity to ask if any of the pupils have seen Paul at all over the last few days."

"Oh, yeah – did you have any luck with finding the school thief, Dad?" Liam asked, suddenly remembering the events of the previous day.

PC Wilson shook his head. "No, but this is far more important."

"I just can't stop thinking about that poor boy, out there, on his own," Mrs Wilson said, shaking her head as she came back into the kitchen. "It doesn't bear thinking about."

Chapter Eight

"Max here is what we call a general purpose police dog," PC Wilson began. "He helps to track down criminals as well as find missing people and property."

Becky nudged Liam proudly as Max sat quietly next to their dad, not moving or making a sound. PC Wilson had requested that his talk take place outside if possible, as there would be more chance of showing exactly what Max could do. So all the classes were seated in rows on the playing field behind the school building. Luckily, it was a fine, warm day.

"Then there are other dogs who are trained to do specialist tasks," PC Wilson went on. "Some look for explosives like bombs; others find illegal drugs. All our dogs begin with basic training, just like any dog might have." He quickly demonstrated how Max could sit, stay, walk, come to heel, and so on.

"The German shepherd is a good police dog for several reasons," PC Wilson explained. "They have highly developed senses, and keep a close eye on everything that's going on."

Everyone laughed as Mrs Mason coughed and Max's ears pricked up.

PC Wilson led Max away from the watching children, told him to sit on the grass, and then walked off. "I'm going to show you just how good Max's hearing is, but I'll need you to be quiet first!"

Everyone's so quiet, you could hear a pin drop, Liam thought with a grin. Max was certainly a hit with Ellandale Primary!

"You can see that I'm now about 60 to 70 metres away from Max," PC Wilson said. Then he lowered his voice to a soft whisper, which even the audience could hardly hear. "Down, Max."

Max immediately lay down on his stomach, dark eyes fixed on his handler.

"Stand," PC Wilson whispered, and Max climbed to his feet. Everyone watched, hardly daring to breathe in case they put Max off.

"Sit." At the next command, Max sat down again.

"That's called distance control." PC Wilson smiled at the look of amazement on the audience's faces. "And it shows just how good Max's hearing is!"

The whole school applauded as Max trotted patiently back to his handler.

"Now I'll show you some of the special things that Max can do." PC Wilson glanced at Liam and Becky's teacher. "Miss Kendall, do you think you could help us out?"

The teacher looked surprised. "Certainly," she agreed.

"I'm going to walk Max to the other end of the field," PC Wilson explained. "Could you go and hide round the corner of the school building out of sight?"

He turned and led Max away at a brisk trot. Miss Kendall hurried off the field towards the school. When the teacher was hidden, PC Wilson brought Max back.

"This is how we find missing people or criminals," he told everyone. "Search and locate, Max!"

Max was immediately on full alert, every muscle tensed. He sniffed the air, and then bounded forward at speed, heading away from the field and towards the school. As everyone craned their necks to see what was happening, Max stopped a little way from the corner of the building and began to bark loudly.

"Well done, Max!" PC Wilson called. "OK, Miss Kendall, you can come out now!"

"I'm glad I'm not a real criminal!" Miss Kendall remarked thankfully as she rejoined her class.

PC Wilson grinned. "Like I said before, Max doesn't just find people, he also locates property. Mrs Mason, could I borrow your scarf, please?"

"Of course," the head teacher agreed. She untied the silky blue scarf from her neck, and handed it over.

PC Wilson took it some way across the field, and hung it out of sight, on the branch of a large tree. "Now let's see if Max can find it!" he said.

Everyone watched intently as Max was sent off across the field to "find". Within a few seconds, he was heading for the tree. And as soon as he reached it, Max began to bark.

There was a gasp of admiration, and everyone clapped loudly. Liam and Becky joined in proudly. Max had done it again!

PC Wilson explained that Max was trained to pick up the scent of humans in unexpected places. "But if there are lots of humans about, it can put a dog off from finding the scent of just one," he went on. "That was why I took the scarf right across the field, away from all of you."

The trick was repeated several times, using another teacher's watch and then a

2p coin. Max found them all easily.

Afterwards, everyone was invited to ask PC Wilson questions. By the time all the questions had been answered, the bell rang for morning playtime.

Mrs Mason thanked PC Wilson for coming. "But before you go off to play, PC Wilson has something he would like to ask you," she added. "It's about Paul Carter, the boy who's gone missing."

Liam and Becky glanced at each other.

"Yes, I'm sure you've all seen the posters around the village," PC Wilson said. "Paul has been spotted near Ellandale, so if anyone else has seen him over the last couple of days, I'd be very interested to hear about it." He looked around as everyone started muttering to each other, but no one put their hand up or said anything.

"Oh, well, maybe Paul will be found today, anyway," Liam sighed as each class stood up in turn, and made their way into the playground.

"Let's hope so," Becky said quietly.

"Right, my class next," called Miss Kendall, who was on playground duty.

Towards the end of playtime, PC Wilson, who'd popped into the staffroom to have a quick cup of coffee, came out into the playground again with Max.

They were immediately mobbed. Everyone was eager to stroke the police dog, who took it all in his stride.

Liam and Becky were dying to go over and fuss over Max themselves, but decided to let everyone else have a chance first. Then, when the bell rang and everyone else left to line up, they rushed over and gave Max a quick fuss.

"You were great, Max!" Becky exclaimed.

Max was thrilled to see them. He swished his tail furiously from side to side, snuggling up against the twins as they both crouched down to hug him.

"You two had better go and line up," PC Wilson said. "Max and I are going to join the search party now."

"Good luck!" said Liam, giving Max a final pat as he walked off with their father. Max wasn't taking much notice, however. He was already sniffing the air and looking around intently.

The twins ran over to join the end of their class's line. But a short sharp bark made them turn round. Max was showing great interest in an old, run-down shed that stood in a corner of the playground.

"Miss Kendall, what's in that shed?" PC Wilson called, looking puzzled.

"Well, nothing really," Miss Kendall replied. Asking another teacher to keep an eye on 6K as they went back into their classroom, Miss Kendall hurried over to PC Wilson. Liam and Becky followed, determined not to miss out on anything. "We don't use it much," the teacher added. "There's some old gym equipment in there, but that's all."

Max was now pawing at the shed door and barking.

PC Wilson examined the lock. "It's broken," he said. "I think I'd better take a look inside."

The twins held their breath as the door creaked open. They all peered in.

"Look!" Liam pointed at the floor. It was littered with chocolate wrappers, crisp bags and empty milk cartons.

Max was pulling his handler towards a dusty pile of gym equipment.

There was a scuffling sound from behind a pile of rickety-looking wooden benches, and then a boy appeared, blinking in the light.

"Paul!" Liam and Becky exclaimed together.

Chapter Nine

"I came to look for Bouncer," Paul muttered, in between mouthfuls of fish fingers, chips and peas. "That's why I ran away."

After Max's amazing discovery, things had moved fast. PC Wilson radioed the police station to let them know that Paul was safe, and that the search could be called off. Then Paul's parents were called, and he was taken back to Lark Cottage for a meal while he waited for them to arrive.

He was sitting there now, with Max at

his side, and the Wilsons listening to his
story. Liam and Becky had pleaded to be
allowed to go back to Lark Cottage with
Paul. As it hadn't been long to lunchtime,
Mrs Mason and Miss Kendall had agreed
– so long as they were back in time for
afternoon registration. Now they were
hanging onto Paul's every word.

"But why did your parents give
Bouncer away?" Liam asked.

Paul's eyes filled with tears.

"Tell us what happened, Paul," PC Wilson said gently.

Paul swallowed hard. "Well, we got Bouncer from an animal shelter," he began. "He's really great, and I love him. But he's very badly behaved. He chewed *everything*. And he kept wrecking the furniture and the carpets. Then the neighbours started to complain because he barked all the time too."

"So your parents just got rid of him!" Liam exclaimed in disgust, then shut up as both his parents gave him a warning look.

"They didn't want to," Paul explained sadly. "They loved Bouncer too, but they said they couldn't cope."

Liam opened his mouth to say something else, but Becky nudged him and he closed it again.

"So we took Bouncer back to the

animal shelter," Paul went on in a wobbly voice. "My mum asked them to let us know when they'd found him a good home. Then they told us that someone in Ellandale was going to adopt him."

"So you came here to try and find him," PC Wilson said gently.

Paul nodded. "I caught the bus here four days ago, and I've been looking for him ever since. I just want to see him again . . ." He bit his lip, struggling to hold back the tears now.

There was silence for a few moments. "I didn't think anyone would look for me in the school shed," Paul went on. "I hoped everyone would think I'd keep right out of the village."

"You were right, Paul," Liam said. "And if it wasn't for Max, you might still be there, miserable and hungry!"

Paul gave him a shaky smile, and nodded. "I noticed the shed when I took the milk and stuff," he explained. Then he looked at PC Wilson and blushed. "Honestly, I've never stolen anything before. But I was so hungry—"

"Don't worry about that now," the policeman said reassuringly. "I'm sure we can sort it out."

Just then, there was the sound of a vehicle pulling up outside.

Paul turned pale. "That'll be Mum and Dad. They're going to be really mad at me – I know they are!"

"I shouldn't worry about that," PC Wilson said. "I think they'll just be happy to see you safe and sound!"

Paul swallowed and nodded, although he still looked tense as PC Wilson got up to open the door. At the same time, Max jumped to his feet and followed his handler, sniffing the air with interest.

"You should ask your mum and dad to let you have your dog back!" Liam said to Paul.

Paul shook his head. "I can't," he sighed. "And anyway, Bouncer's got a new home now."

"Ssh!" Becky said. "What's that?"

They all listened.

Max had bounded ahead to the front door, and was snuffling and sniffing along the bottom of it with great interest. He gave a short, sharp bark. Then the sound of scrabbling and whining came from outside, along with an answering bark.

"Hey, there's another dog out there!" Liam began.

But Paul was already on his feet. "That's Bouncer!" he gasped.

Chapter Ten

As PC Wilson opened the door, a shaggy brown tornado hurtled in. The little dog paused only to have a quick, friendly sniff at Max, before racing down the hallway, barking loudly.

Paul was already running to meet him. "Bouncer!" he yelled. The dog leapt into his arms, yapping with delight. Paul didn't seem to know whether to laugh or cry. "What are you doing here?"

As Paul hugged Bouncer, two people rushed through the front door, pausing only to have a brief word with PC Wilson.

Liam guessed that these were Paul's parents. But why did they have Bouncer with them?

"Paul!" Mrs Carter's face lit up as she caught sight of her son. Both she and Mr Carter looked very pale and heavy-eyed as if they hadn't slept a wink for the last few days. "We've been so worried about you!"

"Sorry, Mum," Paul muttered as both his parents hugged him tightly. Liam and

Becky both beamed as they watched. Meanwhile, Bouncer barked furiously, and Max joined in occasionally.

"Let's all sit down, and I'll put the kettle on," said Tina Wilson with a smile.

Tears in her eyes, Mrs Carter flopped into a chair. She still had an arm around Paul, who was still holding Bouncer.

"Paul, if only you'd told us how much you were missing Bouncer!" Mr Carter said. "We'd have got him back. You shouldn't just have run off like that!"

"Sorry," Paul said guiltily.

"The thing was, we were missing him too!" Mr Carter said. "Even though he *was* so naughty!"

Paul still looked dazed. "But, Mum, why is Bouncer here?" he asked. The little dog was trying to lick every centimetre of Paul's face.

"Well, we rang the animal shelter this morning to see if there was any chance of us getting Bouncer back," Mrs Carter explained. "And it turned out that Mrs Castle, Bouncer's new owner, had called the shelter just a few hours before. She said Bouncer was off his food, and she was worried that he wasn't going to settle with her."

"So Mrs Castle let us have him back." Paul's father was smiling from ear to ear.

Paul's eyes opened wide. "You mean – Bouncer's ours again?"

"He certainly is!" Paul's mother agreed.

"Brilliant!" Becky and Liam exclaimed together, although Paul was too overjoyed to speak. He simply hugged Bouncer even tighter, and buried his face in the dog's shaggy coat.

"You should send Bouncer to training

classes to stop him behaving badly," Liam suggested.

Mr and Mrs Carter looked at him and nodded.

"The animal shelter suggested that too," Paul's father said. "Somehow, we never got around to doing it before. But now we certainly shall!"

Paul finally found his voice again. "Oh, this is brilliant!" he exclaimed happily. He

bent down to pat the German shepherd on the head. "Thank you, Max!"

On Saturday morning, a couple of days later, Max was off-duty, so Becky and Liam took him for a walk through Ellandale.

Everything had worked out for the best. Paul and Bouncer had been reunited and were back home, and Max was now known around Ellandale as the dog who had found the missing boy. He had become a local celebrity.

"It was a good job Max was on the case!" Liam said, ruffling the dog's thick fur. "If it hadn't been for him, Paul might have been missing for ages."

Becky wasn't listening. She nudged Liam. "Isn't that Sergeant Thornton?"

There was a row of stone cottages in front of them with small, flower-filled front gardens. In the very end cottage the policeman was pottering around, dead-heading a clump of white rose bushes.

"That must be where he lives," Liam whispered back.

"Oh, well done, Sherlock Holmes!" Becky grinned. "Let's go and say hello!"

"Why?" Liam wanted to know. "He doesn't like us much!"

"Yes, but he'll have to be nice to us now Max is a hero!" Becky replied with a wink. "Hello, Sergeant Thornton!"

Sergeant Thornton certainly didn't look very pleased to see them. He gave them a grudging nod, and carried on with his gardening.

"Everyone in Ellandale's talking about Max, you know, Sergeant Thornton!" Becky called. "He's going to be in the local newspaper too!"

Sergeant Thornton managed a feeble smile. "*Is* he now?" he muttered. "Well, I suppose he didn't do a bad job – for his first effort. Anyway, I'd better get on." And he turned and went towards the open door of his house.

"I suppose that's about as much praise as Max is going to get!" Becky said as they moved off.

"Oh, he'll change his mind when Max has solved loads more cases!" Liam said confidently.

"Sooty! Sooty! Come here!"

Liam and Becky stopped and looked at one another.

"That's Sergeant Thornton!" Becky whispered. "Who's he calling?"

They both peered through the hedge next door. Sergeant Thornton had come outside with a plate of food, and was looking round the garden.

"Sooty! Lunchtime!" he called.

As Liam and Becky watched, a huge, glossy black cat strolled out from behind a lavender bush. Yawning, it padded across the lawn towards the plate.

"Who's a lovely boy then?" Sergeant Thornton murmured, stroking the cat as it began to eat.

Liam and Becky looked at each other, trying not to giggle.

"How about that!" Becky whispered. "He's just a big softie, really!"

Liam grinned. "I'm so glad we moved here," he said. "Living in Ellandale is going to be *great*, isn't it, Max?"

And Max wagged his tail and woofed in agreement.